To Jane Langton, who has great skills with No-No Birds.
AFP and PP

For Lis, thank you for all your love and constant support.
My love, Jim

First published in Great Britain in 2008 and in the USA in 2009 by
Frances Lincoln Children's Books,
4 Torriano Mews, Torriano Avenue, London NW5 2RZ

www.franceslincoln.com

First paperback edition published in Great Britain and the USA in 2010

A catalogue record for this book is available from the British Library.

ISBN: 978-1-84780-067-1

Printed in Singapore by Tien Wah Press (Pte) Ltd. in November 2009

1 3 5 7 9 8 6 4 2

Andrew Fusek Peters is the tallest author in the UK (6ft 8ins)!
It is te   ıly way he can fit in ideas for new books. For twenty years
he h   ɔeen visiting schools with his digeridoo, performing from
h   ɔoks and twanging his jaw-harp. His previous books for
ɪ   ıces Lincoln include *Animals Aboard,* also illustrated by
Jim Coplestone.

F   ly Peters is not tall at all but she does have a big voice.
Thi   ın be very annoying for her family when she's working on
n   books or poems, because she reads everything out loud
she's writing. However, it comes in very useful when
she and Andrew write together!

Coplestone has worked as a primary school teacher,
aı   ·kshop leader and home-tutor. He loves stories and this is
apr   in his lively and colourful pictures. He lives near the seaside
l his other books for Frances Lincoln are *Noah's Bed,*
S   *a Secret* by Laurence Anholt and *A Walk in the Wild Woods*
by Lis Jones.

The No-No Bird

Andrew Fusek Peters and Polly Peters

Illustrated by Jim Coplestone

F

FRANCES LINCOLN
CHILDREN'S BOOKS

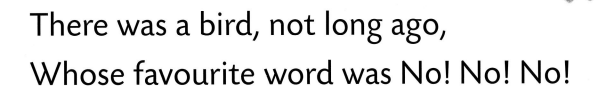

There was a bird, not long ago,
Whose favourite word was No! No! No!

"**No!**" he said to brushing hair,
"**No!**" to coats he wouldn't wear.

So many times he said this word,
That soon his name was No-No Bird.

Well, **No-No Bird** went out one day,
Proudly walking on his way.

Soon, he met a little mouse
Who ran out from her
little house.

"Who are you?" she said. "Do stay,
Would you like to come and play?

But **No-No Bird** just shook his head.
"No! **No! No!**" he loudly said.

"Silly Mouse! Have you not heard?
I'm the famous **No-No Bird!**"

At that, the Mouse began to cry!
"You're very rude," she sniffed,
"GOODBYE."

The path led deeper through the wood
And up ahead, a squirrel stood.

Squirrel saw the bird and said,
"Why walk when you could fly instead?

Let's play catch in that big tree.
I'll chase you and you chase me."

Bird stood still and tapped his toe,
Shook his head and just said, "**No!**"

"Funny Bird," laughed Squirrel, "why?
Is there a problem? Can't you fly?"

But Bird just said, "Have you not heard?
I'm the famous No-No Bird."

And off he walked until a sound
Of **hissing** rose up from the ground.

It was a snake whose smile was wide
Enough to fit a bird inside...

He flicked his tail around Bird's leg,

"Ju-s-s-s-t s-s-stay a moment pleas-s-se, I beg."

No-No Bird stood still and sighed,
"You don't know who I am!"
he cried.

"That's right!" said Snake quite hungrily,
"So tell me now, because, you see,
My favourite food, I'm sure you've heard,
Is quite delicious...

No-No Bird!"

"Ah!" said Bird, "Um. Well. **Oh dear**."

But suddenly his mind was clear.
"The No-No Bird," he said, "is rare.
I haven't seen one anywhere!"

"Hmm," said Snake, "that's such a shame,
But you still haven't said YOUR name."

"Well," said Bird, "I WILL tell you...

...another time!" And up he flew,

Swiftly flapping fast as fear
Straight back home to Mother-dear.

"Goodness! You were quick!" she said.
Bird nodded once, then hung his head.

"I think you'd better come right here
And have a little cuddle, dear!"

And as he climbed upon her knee,
Bird said quietly, "I agree."

Could anyone believe their ears?

Were there tantrums?

Were there tears?

Mother smiled and hugged her bird.
"Do you **still** have a favourite word?"
She asked him as they cuddled tight.
And Bird looked up and said, "I might.

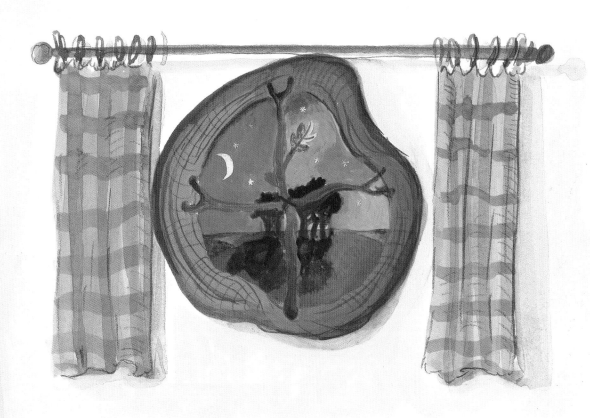

I found out something new today.
I didn't get to stop and play.
I didn't make a single friend,
And nearly met a sticky end."

Bird smiled and said, "So can you guess?
I've changed my favourite word to...

YES!"

MORE TITLES FROM FRANCES LINCOLN CHILDREN'S BOOKS

Animals Aboard
Andrew Fusek Peters
Illustrated by Jim Coplestone

There's a party on the train, now who to invite
To climb aboard and dance through the night?
Sing along as the party starts off slowly, and gets wilder and wilder
before slowing down to a snooze at bedtime. All aboard!

Seven for a Secret
Laurence Anholt
Illustrated by Jim Coplestone

From her apartment in the city, Ruby begins a correspondence
with Grampa, far away in his forest home. Told in letter form
and woven around the ancient rhyme of the magpies, Laurence
Anholt's moving story is about youth and old age, sunshine and
snow, sorrow and joy, birth and death – a song of love and hope.

A Walk in the Wild Woods
Lis Jones
Illustrated by Jim Coplestone

When Ruby and Rabby are together, they aren't scared of many
things, but they are not too sure about going for a walk in the
wild woods… Ruby, Rabby and Daddy set off to the wild woods,
on the look-out for Foxy. They have a lovely time – but Foxy gives
them all a big surprise!

Frances Lincoln titles are available from all good bookshops.
You can also buy books and find out more about your favourite titles,
authors and illustrators on our website: www.franceslincoln.com